for
Deborah Robinson
& Kavita Sapre

Hathi Chiti's
TALES OF **INDIA**

In the Indian Night Sky

Written by Reshma Sapre

Illustrated by Jayme Robinson

Hathi Chiti
Books for Kids

One night, high above India, Sun, Moon and Wind were all getting ready for a big night.

A great feast was being prepared
by their cousins, Thunder and Lightning,
to celebrate the coming of the Rains.

Sun, Moon and Wind all went to their mother,
Star of the North Sky, to tell her of the feast.

Star told her three children that she would stay behind, lighting a bright path to their celebration.

All she asked was that each of her children bring her something from the great feast.

Sun danced around feeling like the most beautiful one,

while Wind boasted about being the strongest,

but Moon remained quiet and gentle. She was just happy to be going to the celebration.

They all bid farewell to their mother and followed her light to Thunder and Lightning's corner of the night sky.

Sun shone brighter than ever, while Moon seemed to glide on Wind's cool breeze.

The feast was glorious. They met many stars and danced all night long with the joyous Rains.

Sun was delighted when the Rains told her she was much brighter than her cousin Lightning.

Wind blew strong breezes for the rains to dance in and Moon looked on, shining with happiness.

Thunder wondered why Star of the North Sky did not join them and Moon pointed to the distant light coming from their side of the night sky. Moon told Thunder that mother had stayed behind to light their way back home.

Sun and Wind celebrated with their new friends, eating all the delicious treats that were put before them.

Moon, remembering her mother's request, collected sweets, bread and wine to carry on her journey back.

Moon gathered Sun and Wind to take them back home.
They were tired and lazy from eating too m... ...ng for too long.

Wind was too tired to blow a strong breeze to help them along and Sun was too dim to light the way.

Moon was grateful to see her mother's light coming from the distance. She followed the light, guiding her brother and sister back home.

When they arrived, Star was delighted to see them. Sun and Wind chattered about how many stars were out and all the things they had done.

Star of the North Sky said she would have liked to see her old friends. Then she asked them to tell her all about the great feast.

Sun and Wind suddenly remembered that their
mother had asked them to bring something back for her.
But they were having so much fun that they had
both forgotten to do so.

Star looked at Moon who was carrying a small bag.

Moon said, "Don't worry, mother,
I have brought you something from all of us."

Star opened the bag of sweets, bread and wine and shone brightly, beaming her light at Moon.

She then turned to Sun and Wind: "I kept watch over all of you while you were celebrating at the feast."

"Sun," she said, "you looked so proud, beaming even brighter than Lightning, but you were too tired to light the way home."

And to Wind she said, "You blew in so many directions for the Rains to dance, and became so tired that your sister had to carry this bag home all alone."

"Moon, you have behaved well. Thank you for bringing me this small taste of the celebrations; for this, you will be rewarded."

Both Sun and Wind nervously waited to hear what their mother would say to them.

"Sun, my child, you shall be the brightest star in the sky; but you shall be so hot that people will cover their heads when they walk under you."

"Wind, my child, you are the strong one, and from this day on you will blow mightily in hot, dry weather, but you will whip the Rains about when they come."

"All creatures big and small will hide from you, waiting for you to pass."

"Moon, for remembering your old mother
and bringing your brother and sister home safely,

you will always be cool and light, calming the night sky
when you make your appearance.
People will look upon you as one who is blessed."

Moon, feeling very happy, thanked Star,
but she also felt bad for her sister and brother.
She thought for a moment, then asked her mother,

"How will I enjoy myself when
my brother and sister must suffer so?"

To this, her mother replied, "Moon, when you shine bright and full, you will keep Sun company day and night. And when you are full and bright, people will rejoice at the shimmering Rains dancing to Wind's breeze in your silvery light."

Sun and Wind rejoiced. They knew they would not be alone because their sister Moon would always accompany them. All three danced happily together, while Star feasted on the wonderful food brought back from the celebration.

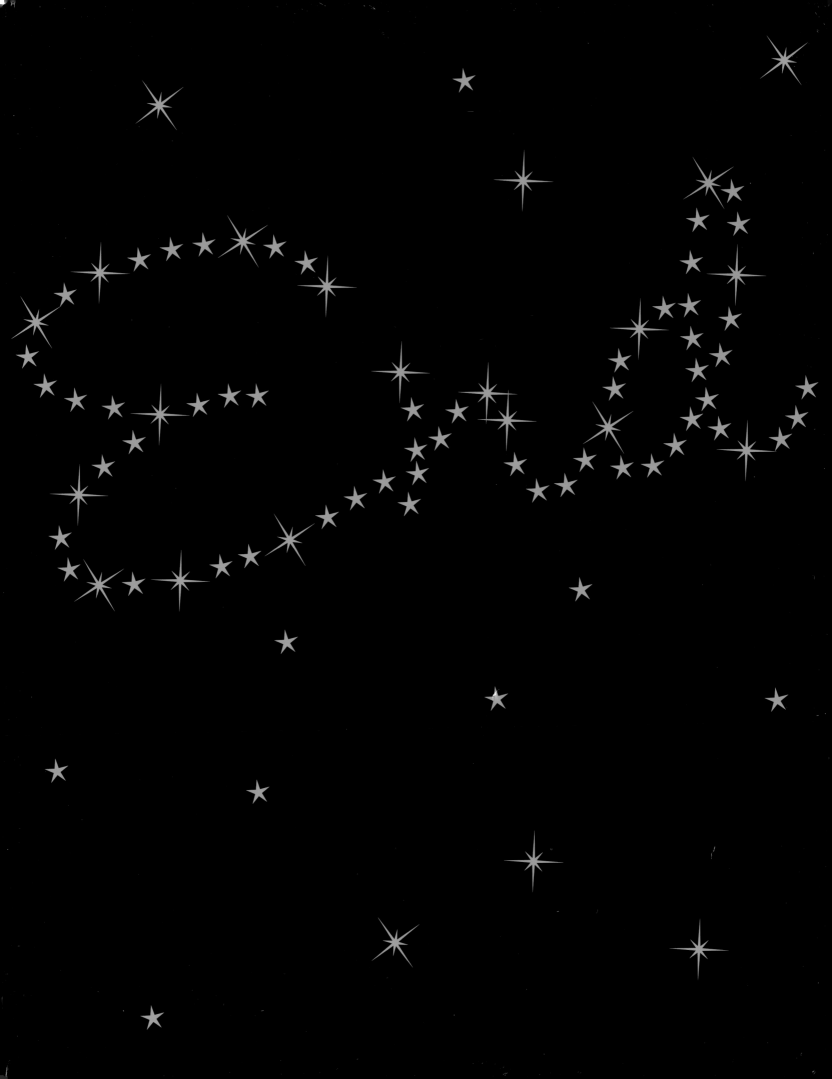

This edition published in 2010 by
Hathi Chiti Books for Kids
PO Box 1219
New York, NY 10016
USA
info@HathiChiti.com
www.HathiChiti.com

First published in India in 2007 by Mapin Publishing
in association with HarperCollins Children's Books,
an imprint of HarperCollins Publishers India

Text and illustrations
© Hathi Chiti Books for Kids

ISBN: 978-0-615-37072-9
Library of Congress Catalog-in-Publication Data on file.
Typeset in Scrawl
Printed in China